21

1/15

9/20

The dragon coiled around Byron.

THE SPIDERWICK CHRONICLES

CHRONICLES

THE WRATH OF MULGARATH

BOOK FIVE OF FIVE

Tony DiTerlizzi *and* Holly Black

Simon and Schuster Books for Young Readers

New York   London   Toronto   Sydney

SIMON & SCHUSTER BOOKS FOR YOUNG READERS
An imprint of Simon & Schuster Children's Publishing Division
1230 Avenue of the Americas, New York, New York 10020

This jacketed movie tie-in edition January 2008

10 9 8 7 6 5 4 3 2

CIP data for this book is available from the Library of Congress.
ISBN 0-689-85940-6

Jacketed edition ISBN-13: 978-1-4169-5021-9
Jacketed edition ISBN-10: 1-4169-5021-4

For my grandmother, Melvina,
who said I should write a book just like this one
and to whom I replied that I never would
—H. B.

For Arthur Rackham,
may you continue to inspire others
as you have me
—T. D.

Table of Contents

List of Full-Page Illustrations

Dear Reader,

Over the years that Tony and I have been
friends, we've shared the same childhood
fascination with faeries. We did not realize
the importance of that bond or how it might be
tested.

One day Tony and I—along with several other
authors—were doing a signing at a large bookstore.
When the signing was over, we lingered, helping
to stack books and chatting, until a clerk
approached us. He said that there had been a
letter left for us. When I inquired which one of
us, we were surprised by his answer.

"Both of you," he said.

The letter was exactly as reproduced on the
following page. Tony spent a long time just
staring at the photocopy that came with it.
Then, in a hushed voice, he wondered aloud about
the remainder of the manuscript. We hurriedly
wrote a note, tucked it back into the envelope,
and asked the clerk to deliver it to the Grace
children.

Not long after, a package arrived on my
doorstep, bound in red ribbon. A few days after
that, three children rang the bell and told me
this story.

What has happened since is hard to describe.
Tony and I have been plunged into a world we
never quite believed in. We now see that faeries
are far more than childhood stories. There is an
invisible world around us and we hope that you,
dear reader, will open your eyes to it.

HOLLY BLACK

Dear Mrs. Black and Mr. DiTerlizzi:

I know that a lot of people don't believe in faeries, but I do and I think that you do too. After I read your books, I told my brothers about you and we decided to write. We know about real faeries. In fact, we know a lot about them.

The page attached* to this one is a photocopy from an old book we found in our attic. It isn't a great copy because we had some trouble with the copier. The book tells people how to identify faeries and how to protect themselves. Can you please give this book to your publisher? If you can, please put a letter in this envelope and give it back to the store. We will find a way to send the book. The normal mail is too dangerous.

We just want people to know about this. The stuff that has happened to us could happen to anyone.

Sincerely,

Mallory, Jared, and Simon Grace

*Not included.

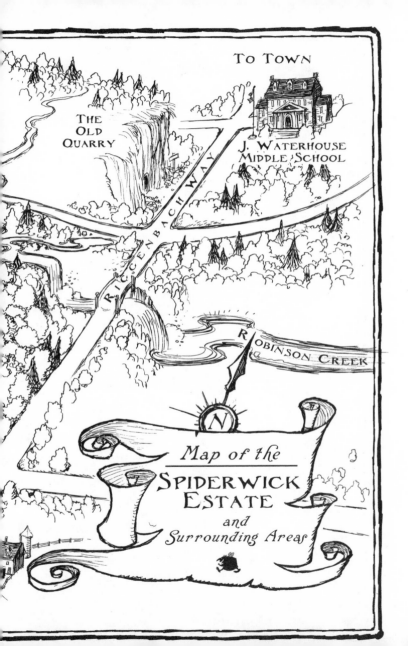

At the gate of the Spiderwick estate

Chapter One

IN WHICH the World
Is Turned Upside Down

The pale light of the newly risen sun made the dew shimmer on the nearby grass as Jared, Mallory, and Simon trudged along the early morning roads. They were tired, but the need to get home kept them going. Mallory shivered in her thin white dress, clutching her sword so hard that her knuckles went white. Beside her, Simon shuffled along, kicking stray bits of asphalt. Jared was quiet too. Each time his eyes closed, even for a moment, all he saw were goblins—hundreds of goblins, with Mulgarath at their head.

Jared tried to distract himself by planning what he would say to his mother when they finally got home. She was going to be furious with them for being gone all night and even madder at Jared because of that thing with the knife. But he could explain everything now. He imagined telling her about the shape-shifting ogre, the rescue of Mallory from the dwarves, and the way they had tricked the elves. His mother would look at the sword and she would have to believe them. And then she would forgive Jared for everything.

A sharp sound, like a tea kettle whistling at full volume, snapped him back to the present. They were at the gate of the Spiderwick estate. To Jared's horror, trash, papers, feathers, and broken furniture littered the lawn.

"What is all that?" Mallory gasped.

A screech drew Jared's eyes upward, where

Simon's griffin was chasing a small creature around the roof and knocking pieces of slate loose. Stray feathers drifted over the roof tiles.

"Byron!" Simon called, but the griffin either didn't hear or chose to ignore him. Simon turned to Jared in exasperation. "He shouldn't be up there. His wing is still hurt."

"What's he after?" Mallory asked, squinting.

"A goblin, I think," said Jared slowly. The memory of teeth and claws red with blood awakened a horrible dread within him.

"Mom!" Mallory gasped, and began to run toward the house.

Jared and Simon raced after her. Up close they could see that the windows of the old estate were smashed and the front door hung by a single hinge.

They darted inside, through the mudroom, stepping over scattered keys and torn coats. In the kitchen, water poured from the faucet, filling a sink piled with broken plates and spilling onto the floor, where food from the overturned freezer was defrosting in wet piles. The wallboard had been punched open in places, and plaster dust, mingling with spilled flour and cereal, covered the stove.

The dining room table was still upright, but several of the chairs were knocked over, their caning ripped. One of their great-uncle's paintings was slashed and the frame was cracked, although it still hung on the wall.

The living room was worse: The television was shattered and their game console had been shoved through it. The sofas were ripped open, and stuffing was scattered across the floorboards like drifts of snow. And there, sitting on the remains of a brocade footstool, was Thimbletack.

"All my fault, all my fault."

As Jared moved closer to the little brownie, he could see that Thimbletack had a long, raw scratch on his shoulder and that his hat was missing. He blinked up at Jared with wet, black eyes.

"All my fault, all my fault," Thimbletack said. "I tried to fight; my magic's too slight." A tear rolled down his thin cheek, and he wiped it away angrily. "Goblins alone I might have driven off. The ogre just looked at me and scoffed."

"Where's Mom?" Jared demanded. He could feel himself trembling.

"Just before the break of day, they bound her and carried her away," Thimbletack said.

"They *can't* have!" Simon's voice was close to a squeak. "Mom!" he called, rushing to the stairs and shouting up to the next landing. *"Mom!"*

"We have to do something," said Mallory.

"We *saw* her," Jared said softly, sitting down on the ruined couch. He felt light-headed, and hot and cold at the same time. "At the quarry. She was the adult the goblins had with them. Mulgarath had her, and we didn't even notice. We should have listened—*I* should have listened. I never should have opened Uncle Arthur's stupid book."

The brownie shook his head vigorously. "To protect the house and those inside is *my* duty, Guide or no Guide."

"But if I had destroyed it like you said, none of this would have happened!" Jared punched himself in the leg.

Thimbletack scrubbed his eyes with the heel of

his hand. "No one knows if that is true or not. I hid it away—see what we got?"

"Enough with the pity party—neither of you is helping!" Mallory squatted beside the footstool, handing the brownie his hat. "Where would they have taken Mom?"

Thimbletack shook his head sadly. "Goblins are filthy things, the master worse than his hirelings. They would dwell somewhere as foul as they, but where that is, I cannot say."

From above them there was a whistle and a clatter.

"One goblin is still on the roof," said Simon, looking up. "It must know!"

Jared stood up. "We'd better stop Byron before he eats it."

"Right," said Simon, heading up the stairs.

The three kids ran up the steps and down the hall toward the attic. The bedroom doors on

the second floor were open. Torn clothing, pillow feathers, and ripped bedding spilled out
into the hall. Outside Jared and Simon's shared
room, cracked, empty tanks lay on the floor.
Simon froze, a stricken expression on his face.

"Lemondrop?" Simon called. "Jeffrey?
Kitty?"

"Come on," Jared said. As he steered Simon
away from the wreckage of their room, he
caught sight of the hall closet. The shelves were
dripping with lotions and shampoos, which
had also soaked the scattered towels. And at
the bottom, near deep scratches in the wallboard, the secret door to Arthur's library had
been ripped off its hinges.

"How did they find it?" Mallory asked.

Simon shook his head. "I guess they ran-
sacked the place looking for it."

Jared crouched down and wriggled into

Arthur Spiderwick's library. Bright sunlight streaming through the single window showed the damage clearly. Tears burned his eyes as he stepped across a carpet of shredded pages. Arthur's books had been ripped free of their bindings and scattered. Torn sketches and toppled bookshelves littered the floor. Jared looked around the room helplessly.

"Well?" Mallory called.

"Destroyed," Jared said. "Everything's destroyed."

"Come on," Simon called. "We have to get that goblin."

Jared nodded his head, despite the fact that neither his brother nor his sister could see him, and moved numbly toward the door. There was something about the desecration of this one room—a room that had remained secret all these years—that made Jared feel as

"Everything's destroyed."

though nothing would ever be right again.

Together he, Simon, and Mallory trudged up the stairs to the attic, crossing over glittering pieces of smashed holiday ornaments and stepping past a broken dress form. In the dim light Jared could see dust erupting in time with the clattering of griffin claws, and he could hear more screeching above them.

"One more level and we can step right onto the roof," Jared said, pointing to the final staircase. It led to the single highest room in the house, a small tower with half-boarded windows on all four sides.

"I think I heard some barking," Simon said as they climbed. "That goblin must still be okay."

When they reached the top of the tower, Mallory swung her sword at the window boards, splintering them. Jared tried to pry off what was left loose.

"I'll go first," Simon said, hopping onto the ledge and gingerly climbing past the jagged slats and onto the roof.

"Wait!" Jared shouted. "What makes you think you can control that griffin?" But Simon didn't seem to be paying attention.

Mallory strapped on a belt, wrapping it around the sword so it hung from her hip. "Come on!"

Jared swung his legs over the sill and stepped out onto the slate. The sudden sunlight almost blinded him, and for a moment his blurry eyes scanned the forest beyond their lawn.

Then he saw Simon approaching the griffin, who had cornered the goblin against one of the brick chimneys. The goblin was Hogsqueal.

"Stop gawping, snail-heads!"

Chapter Two

IN WHICH an Old Friend Returns

Stop gawping, snail-heads!" Hogsqueal yelled. "Help me!" He was backed against a chimney, one hand holding his coat closed over a largish object, the other brandishing an empty slingshot menacingly.

"Hogsqueal?" Jared grinned at the sight of the hobgoblin, then stopped with a scowl. "What are you doing here?"

Simon was holding the griffin back, mostly by standing between him and Hogsqueal and yelling loudly. Byron turned his hawk head to the side and blinked, then pawed the ground with his talons as though he were more feline than bird. Jared suspected that Byron thought they were playing a new game.

Hogsqueal hesitated, seeing Jared's face. "I didn't know this was *your* house until the griffin showed up."

"You helped catch our mother?" Jared could feel his face growing warm. "Trash our house? Kill Simon's pets?" He took two steps toward Hogsqueal, hands fisting. He'd *trusted* Hogsqueal. He'd *liked* him. And the hobgoblin had *betrayed* them. Jared could barely think with the roaring in his ears.

"I didn't kill anything." Hogsqueal opened his coat a little, revealing a marmalade ball of fur.

"Kitty!" Simon said, distracted by the sight of the kitten.

In that moment Byron lunged past Simon,

catching the hobgoblin's arm in his beak.

"Aaaaaaahhhhh!" Hogsqueal screamed. The cat yowled, jumping onto the roof.

"Byron, no!" Simon yelled. "Drop him!"

The griffin shook his head, whipping Hogsqueal back and forth. The hobgoblin's shouts became louder.

"Do something!" Jared called, panicked.

Simon stepped up to the griffin and hit him hard on the beak with his hand. "NO!" he shouted.

"Oh crap, don't do *that*!" Mallory said, reaching for the sword at her waist. But instead of attacking, the griffin stopped shaking Hogsqueal and looked at Simon with something like alarm.

"Drop him!" Simon repeated, pointing to the slate roof.

Hogsqueal struggled ineffectually, pushing

"I'm sorry, gobstoppers."

his fingers into Byron's nose slits and trying to bite the feathery neck with his baby teeth. The griffin ignored the hobgoblin but didn't make a move to put him down either.

"Be careful," Jared told his brother. "Better he eats Hogsqueal than us."

"Noooo! I'm sorry, gobstoppers," Hogsqueal said, still writhing. "I didn't mean it! Honest. Get me out of here! Heeeeeelp!"

"Jared," Simon said. "Grab Hogsqueal, okay?"

Jared nodded, edging nearer. This close, he could smell the griffin — it had a feral scent, like a cat's fur.

Simon put one hand on the top of Byron's beak, the other on the bottom, and started to lever them apart, repeating, "Be a gooooood boy. Yes. Drop the goblin."

"*Hob*goblin!" Hogsqueal yelped.

"Are you crazy?" Mallory hollered at her brother. The griffin turned his head abruptly in her direction, almost knocking Simon sprawling.

"Sorry," Mallory said in a much smaller voice.

Jared gripped Hogsqueal around the legs. "Got him."

"Hey, yaffner, we're not going to be playing tug-of-war with my body, right? Right?"

Jared just smiled grimly.

Simon tried again to push Byron's beak open. "Mallory, come and help me. Grab the bottom of the beak, and I'll get the top."

She stepped carefully across the slanted roof. The griffin eyed her nervously.

"When I say pull," Simon said, *"pull."*

Together they tried to pry the griffin's jaws apart. Mallory's fingers slid into Byron's mouth as she strained, nearly hanging from the griffin, trying to use her weight against him. Byron struggled and then suddenly gave in, opening his mouth and dropping Hogsqueal's full weight into Jared's arms. Losing his balance, Jared slid backward on the shingles, letting go of Hogsqueal and scrabbling for a handhold. The hobgoblin slid as well, knocking loose the shingle Jared was gripping on to. Jared slipped and grabbed hold of the gutter moments before he would have fallen off the side of the house.

Simon and Mallory looked at Jared with wide eyes. He swallowed hard. As they moved to haul him back onto the roof, Jared saw Hogsqueal make for the open window.

"He's getting away!" Jared said, trying to pull himself higher. His elbow dug into the dried leaves and mud that clotted the gutter.

"Forget about the stupid goblin," Mallory said. "Grab hold of me."

They hauled him back onto the roof. As soon as he was upright, Jared ran after Hogsqueal with Mallory and Simon close behind. They thundered down the stairs.

Hogsqueal was sprawled in the hall outside their bedrooms, and yellow yarn was wrapping itself around him. Jared gaped as the yarn tied itself in a bow.

Thimbletack hopped up on Hogsqueal's head. "I will help you fight the fey. I believe I've a debt to pay."

Jared looked at the yarn and then back at Thimbletack. "I didn't know you could do that!" He remembered how his shoelaces had seemed to tie themselves together and suddenly had an explanation.

The little brownie grinned. "Being unseen

"He's getting away!"

is not enough to get things clean."

"Hey," Hogsqueal yelled. "Get this crazy kipper off me! I wasn't running out on you. I was escaping from that tooby monster on the roof!"

"Shut up," Mallory said.

"That goblin is not misunderstood," said Thimbletack. "He is just plain no good."

"That noddy brownie's a fine one to talk," said Hogsqueal.

"You're going to tell us everything you know, or we're going to spread ketchup on you and put you right back up on the roof," said Jared. Right then he was so angry that he meant every word of it.

Thimbletack jumped down onto the leg of an overturned coffee table. "That would be overly kind to a goblin in a bind. No, we'll set rats to nibble off your toes, poke out your eyes, and put them up your nose. Your fingers we'll remove with dull scissors, and we'll wait until your confidence withers."

Simon paled but said nothing.

Hogsqueal squirmed in his bindings. "I'll tell you already, surly-boots. No need to threaten!"

"Where is our mom?" Jared demanded. "Where would they have taken her?"

"Mulgarath's lair is at the dump on the edge of town. He's built a palace of trash, and it's defended by his goblin army and by other things besides. Don't be a pumpkin-head.

There is no way you can get in there."

"What other things are defending it?" Jared demanded.

"Dragons," Hogsqueal said. "Little ones, mostly."

"Dragons?" Jared repeated in horror. Arthur's field guide had notes on dragons, but Arthur himself had never seen one. All of his accounts were secondhand. But even second-hand, the stories were frightening—they described poisonous venom, teeth as sharp as daggers, and bodies that were as quick as whips.

"And you were part of Mulgarath's goblin army?" Mallory asked, eyes narrowed.

"I had to be!" Hogsqueal exclaimed. "Everyone was joining up! Where was I sup-posed to go, chatter-basket?"

"What did you tell them happened to the

other goblins—the ones you were with before?"

"*Other* goblins?" Hogsqueal said. "For the last time, lily-pants, I'm a *hob*goblin! You might as well call a blackbird a crow!"

Jared sighed. "So, what *did* you say?"

Hogsqueal rolled his eyes. "What do you think, beetle-guts? I said a troll ate 'em, simple as that."

"If we untie you, will you take us to the dump?" Mallory demanded.

"Probably too late." Hogsqueal grunted.

"What was that?" Jared scowled.

"Yes," Hogsqueal said. "*Yes!* I'll take you. Are you happy, snotters? Just as long as I don't have to see that griffin again."

"But, Jared," Simon said, a small smile twisting his mouth, "it would be a lot faster if we flew."

"Wait, now! I didn't agree to that!" Hogsqueal exclaimed.

"We need a plan," Mallory said, stepping away from the hobgoblin and lowering her voice. "How can we beat an army of goblins, a dragon, and a shape-shifting ogre?"

"There has to be something," said Jared, following her. "They must have a weakness." The pages of Arthur's Guide that had once been so clear in his mind had faded, his memory growing increasingly spotty. He tried to concentrate, to remember anything that might be important.

"Too bad we don't have the field guide." Simon stared at the broken fish tanks as though some answer could be found among the glass shards.

"But we know where Arthur is," said Jared carefully, a plan starting to form in his mind. "We could ask him."

"Just how are you suggesting we do that?" Mallory asked, one hand on her hip.

"I'm going to ask the elves to let me talk to him." Jared spoke as though that were a perfectly reasonable suggestion.

Mallory's eyes widened with surprise. "The last time we saw the elves, they weren't exactly what I would call *friendly*."

"Yeah, they wanted to trap me underground forever," said Simon.

"You have to trust me," Jared said slowly. "I can do it. They promised that they wouldn't hold me there against my will ever again."

"I trust *you*," said Mallory. "It's the elves I don't trust, and you shouldn't either. I'm going to come."

Jared shook his head. "There isn't enough time. Get Hogsqueal to tell you everything he knows about Mulgarath. I'll be back as soon as I can." He looked down at the little brownie. "I'll bring Thimbletack—if he'll come."

"I thought it had to be just you," said Simon.

"I have to be the only human," Jared said, his eyes still fixed on Thimbletack.

"I have not been out of the house in years." With that, Thimbletack walked to the edge of the chair and let Jared put him into the hood

of Jared's sweatshirt. "But I must put aside my fears."

They left before Simon or Mallory could talk them out of it. Crossing the street, they started up the hill toward the elven grove. The late-morning sky had deepened to a bright, cloudless blue, and Jared hurried, afraid that they didn't have much time.

"It is true I took the book."

Chapter Three

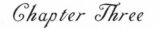

IN WHICH Jared Finds Out Things
He Doesn't Want to Know

The grove was the same as he remembered it—tree-rimmed with mushrooms in the center—but this time when Jared stepped into the middle, nothing happened. No branches laced together to trap him, no roots wound around his ankles, and no elves appeared to scold him.

"Hello!" Jared yelled. He waited a moment, but the only reply was the distant calling of birds.

Frustrated, Jared paced back and forth. "Is

THE GREEN-EYED ELF

anyone here? I'm kind of in a hurry!"

Still nothing. Minutes passed.

Looking at the ring of mushrooms, he had an overwhelming urge to strike out at the elves. If only they hadn't taken Arthur.

He'd just lifted his foot to kick one when he heard a soft voice from the tree line.

"Reckless child, what are you doing in this place?" It was the green-eyed female elf, her hair tinged with more reds and browns than it had been before. And her gown was now deep amber and gold, like summer giving way to fall. Her voice sounded more sad than angry.

"Please," Jared said. "Mulgarath has my mother. I have to save her. You have to let me talk to Arthur."

"What should I care for one mortal?" She turned toward the trees. "Do you know how many of my own people have been lost? How many dwarves—old as the stones beneath our feet—are no more?"

"I saw it," Jared said. "We were there. Please—I'll give you anything. I'll stay here if you want."

She shook her head. "The only thing you had that was of value to us is lost."

Jared felt relief and terror at the same time. He needed to see Arthur, but he had nothing else to offer. "We didn't have the Guide," he said. "We couldn't have given it to you then, but maybe we can get it back now."

The green-eyed elf turned back with a

scowl. "I have no further interest in your tales."

"I . . . I can prove it." Jared reached back into his hood, pulled out Thimbletack, and set him down in the grass. "I told you our house brownie had the book. This is Thimbletack."

The little brownie took off his hat and made a low bow, trembling slightly. "Great Lady, I know how this must look, but it is true I took the book."

"Your manners become you." She glanced at them both and then was silent for a moment.

Jared shifted impatiently as Thimbletack climbed up Jared's leg and slid back into his hiding place. The green-eyed elf's silence unnerved Jared, but he forced himself to stay quiet. This might be their last chance to convince her.

Finally she continued. "Our time to punish and to command is past. The moment we feared is upon us. Mulgarath has gathered a great army and is using the Guide to make it even more fearsome."

Jared nodded, although he was puzzled. He couldn't think of anything Mulgarath could do with the Guide that would make an army more dangerous. It was just a book.

"Promise me this, mortal child," the green-eyed elf said. "If Arthur's field guide comes again into your possession while you look for your mother, you will give it to us so

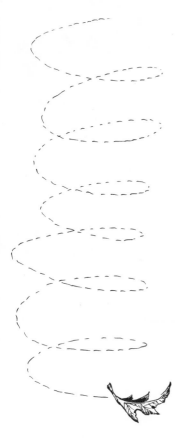

that it can be destroyed."

Jared nodded, giddily agreeing to anything that meant he would be able to see Arthur. "I will. I'll bring it—"

"No," she said. "When it is time, we will come to you." She pointed upward and spoke something in a strange language. A single leaf spiraled from a high branch of an old oak. It drifted slowly, as though it were falling through water instead of air. "Your audience with Arthur Spiderwick will last as long as it takes that leaf to fall to the ground."

Jared looked up toward where she pointed. As slowly as the leaf was moving, it still seemed too fast. "What if that isn't enough time?"

She smiled coldly. "Time is something that neither of us has the luxury of anymore, Jared Grace." But Jared barely noticed, because walking toward them from the trees was a man in a tweed coat, with graying patches of hair on the sides of his balding head. Leaves swept around him and dropped in a carpet in front of him so that his feet never touched the ground. He adjusted his spectacles nervously and peered at Jared.

Jared could not help grinning. Arthur Spiderwick looked just like the picture in the library. Now everything would be all right. His great-great-uncle would explain what to do, and that would be that.

"Uncle Arthur," Jared began. "I'm Jared."

A man in a tweed coat

"I do not believe I could possibly be your uncle, child," Arthur said stiffly. "To the best of my knowledge, my sister has no sons whatso-ever."

"Well, actually, you're my great-great-uncle," Jared said, suddenly unsure of himself. "But that's not important."

"That's nonsense."

This wasn't going the way it was supposed to at all. "You've been gone a long time," Jared explained carefully.

Arthur scowled. "A few months, perhaps."

Thimbletack spoke up, climbing out of his hiding place and onto Jared's shoulder. "Listen to the boy—it is the only way. We cannot afford to delay."

Arthur peered down at the brownie and blinked twice. "Hello, old man! How I have missed you! Is my Lucy well? What about my

41

wife? Will you give them a message for me?"

"Listen!" Jared interrupted. "Mulgarath has my mother, and you're the only one who knows what to do."

"Me?" Arthur asked. "Why should I know what to do?" He pushed his spectacles higher. "I would imagine that I would advise—wait, how old are you?"

"Nine," Jared replied, dreading what would come next.

"I would say that you should stay safe and leave the handling of such dangerous creatures to your elders."

"Didn't you hear me?" Jared shouted. "MULGARATH HAS MY MOTHER! THERE ARE NO ELDERS!"

"I understand," Arthur said. "However, you must—"

"No, you *don't* understand!" Jared couldn't

stop himself. It felt too good to finally just scream at someone. "You don't even know how long you've been here! Lucinda is older than you now! You don't know *anything*."

Arthur opened his mouth as if to speak and then closed it. He looked pale and shaky, but Jared found it hard to care. His eyes burned with unshed tears. On the other side of the ring of mushrooms the single leaf was drifting ever closer to the ground.

"Mulgarath is a very dangerous ogre," Arthur said quietly. He didn't look at Jared when he spoke. "Even the elves do not know how to stop him."

"He has a dragon, too," Jared said.

Arthur looked up suddenly with interest. "A dragon? Really?" Then he shook his head and his shoulders slumped. "I can't tell you how to deal with any of this. I'm sorry—I simply don't know."

Jared wanted to plead, to demand, but no words came.

Arthur took a step closer, and when he

spoke, his voice was very gentle. "Child, if I always knew what to do, would I be here, trapped with the elves, never to see my own family again?"

"I guess not," Jared said, closing his eyes. The leaf had reached his height. It wouldn't be long now before his time was up.

"I can't give you a solution," Arthur said. "All I can give you is information. I wish I could do more."

He continued. "Goblins run in small packs, usually no more than ten. They follow Mulgarath because they're afraid of him — otherwise you would never see so many in one place. Without him leading them, they would fall into squabbling. But even with him, they probably aren't very organized.

"As for ogres, Mulgarath is typical of their kind. They're master shape-shifters — clever, sly,

and cruel. Strong, too, unfortunately. One flaw that might help you is that they are often vain and prone to bragging."

"Like in the 'Puss in Boots' story?" Jared asked.

"Exactly." Arthur's eyes gleamed as he spoke. "Ogres think a lot of themselves and want you to think a lot of them as well. They love to hear themselves talk. And the normal protections—like that garment you're wearing—are next to useless. They're too powerful.

"As for dragons . . . well, I must confess everything I know about them was culled from other researchers."

"Other researchers? You mean there are other people researching faeries?"

Arthur nodded. "All over the world. Did you know there are faeries on every continent? There are variations, of course, much like with any other animal. But I digress.

"The subtype of dragon is probably of the European wyrm variety most common to this region. Very poisonous. I remember one account where a dragon lived on cow's milk — it got huge and its venom poisoned everything, scorched the grass, and made the water undrinkable."

"Wait!" Jared exclaimed. "Our water burns your mouth if you drink it — our well water."

"A very bad sign." Arthur sighed heavily and shook his head. "Dragons are quick, but they can be killed the same as any other crea- ture. The difficulty, of course, is the poison. It

"A very bad sign."

grows stronger as the dragon grows, and only a very small number of creatures are fast enough and brave enough to go after a dragon, the way a mongoose attacks a cobra."

Jared looked at the leaf—it was almost to the ground. Arthur followed the look. "My time talking to you is almost done. Will you give Lucinda a message for me?"

"Sure. Of course." Jared nodded.

"Tell her—" But whatever Arthur was going to say was lost in the leaves that whorled around him, obscuring him from view. A tornado of leaves circled upward and then . . . nothing. Jared looked for the elf, but she was gone as well.

As Jared left the boundary of the grove, he saw Byron clawing in the dirt. Simon sat on the griffin's back, petting the creature to calm it. Behind him, Mallory held the dwarven sword

"It's your turn to trust us."

aloft, the metal gleaming in the sun. Hogsqueal sat at the beast's neck, looking positively miserable.

"What are you doing here?" Jared asked. "I thought you said you trusted me."

"And we do," said Mallory. "That's why we waited here instead of rushing in and hauling you out."

"We even have a plan." Simon held up a loop of rope. "Come on. You can tell us what you found out from the elves on the way."

"So, now," said Mallory, "it's your turn to trust us."

"I caught the humans."

Chapter Four

IN WHICH Everything Goes into the Fire

As he crossed the highway, Jared tried not to jostle the deliberately loose knots that kept his hands bound behind his back. He marched behind a similarly bound Mallory and avoided looking up at the distant shadow of Byron and Simon flying overhead—their only means of escape if things were to go wrong and the quickest way out if things were to go right.

Hogsqueal poked Jared with the tip of the dwarven sword. "Hurry up, nose pickers."

"Cut it out," Jared said, nearly stumbling.

Thimbletack squirmed against the back of his neck. "We're not even inside yet, and that thing is sharp," Jared said.

"Right," the hobgoblin snickered. "My bad, lump-meat."

"Leave Jared alone, or I'm going to *show* you how to use a sword," Mallory hissed, then suddenly went still.

The trees on that side of the highway were almost entirely leafless, blackened, and dead. The few remaining leaves hung from the branches like bats. The trees looked less real than the dwarves' ironwood trees. Just beyond, Jared could see the junkyard.

The gate was rusted open, and the worn dirt path was overgrown with patches of dead weeds. A NO TRESPASSING sign was stuck in the ground at an odd angle. Old cars, tires, and other trash were stacked in haphazard piles

that resembled swells of sand along a beach. And ahead Jared could see the palace clearly. Its spires gleamed with glass and tin in the full light of the sun.

Jared saw several goblins peering out of the rusted heap of a car. Two sniffed the air and a third began to bark. Then the goblins started to crawl from the vehicle. Each lifted a toadlike head and gnashed teeth of glass and bone. They carried dwarf-forged pikes and curved swords.

"You say you captured both?"

"Say something," Jared whispered to Hogsqueal.

"I caught the humans," Hogsqueal called. "No thanks to you trash hounds!"

A large goblin scuttled closer. His teeth were made of bottle glass, and they shimmered in the sunlight—brown, green, and clear. He was dressed in a ragged coat with tarnished buttons and a frayed tricornered hat. The hat in particular caught Jared's eye because it was dyed a strange ruddy brown. Flies buzzed close. "You say *you* captured both?"

"Easily, O large Wormrat," Hogsqueal bragged. "There they were, the girl swinging around this sword right here—sharp, isn't it?—but I was too fast for them! I . . ." Wormrat eyed him, and the hobgoblin's words trailed off. "Okay," he started again. "They were sleeping and I—"

The goblins began to bark loudly. Whether it was laughter or something else, Jared wasn't sure.

"I still caught the scallywags! They're *my* prisoners," Hogsqueal said, raising Mallory's sword. It looked huge in his small hands and was wobbling slightly.

Wormrat barked, and the tip of the sword drooped. Jared glanced upward to see if Simon and Byron were nearby, but they were either well hidden or gone. Jared hoped for what seemed like the millionth time that Simon would be able to control the griffin.

"We do what *I* say," said Wormrat. "Bring them!"

Mallory and Jared were pushed and pulled through the junkyard by a barking mass of goblins. They had to be careful not to step on the jagged pieces of metal that stuck up from the dry dirt at odd angles. Whenever Mallory and Jared slowed, the goblins shoved them and poked them with weapons. Rust from the cars streaked Jared's jeans as he squeezed through the narrow passageways between them. Finally they were led into a clearing where a dozen more goblins were lazing around a fire. Smallish bones were scattered among the debris.

Wormrat grunted and pointed toward a blue car close to the fire. "Tie the prisoners there."

"We should take them to the Palace of Trash," Hogsqueal said, but he sounded halfhearted.

"Quiet!" barked the big goblin. "*I* give commands."

A grinning goblin used a coil of rusty wire to attach Jared and Mallory's tether to the car. As the goblin wrapped the cord around the side mirror, Jared could smell his rotten breath and could see his strange, mottled skin, the hair tufting from his ears, the dead white of his eyes, and the long, quivering whiskers that stuck up from his face. The other goblins stood in a circle, leering and waiting.

"Back to your posts, lazy dogs!" bellowed the large goblin. Then, turning to the goblins that had already been there when he arrived, he scowled. "And the prisoners had better be where I leave them! I go report them to Mulgarath!" Barking, most of his goblins trickled back to their patrols as he left, but a few remained behind to sit around the fire.

Jared wriggled his hands. He was sure the knots were still loose enough for him to get free, but he was less sure they were going to be able to get past all of those goblins.

Jared and Mallory sat in the cold, sandy dirt for what felt like hours, watching the goblins pick up small lizards and toss them into the fire. The sky began to darken, the sun lighting slashes of gold across the waning day.

"Maybe this wasn't such a great plan after all," Mallory said softly. "We're nowhere near Mom, and I don't know where Simon is."

"But we're almost there," Jared whispered back. Their hands were close enough that he could take one of hers and squeeze it.

"What are they waiting for?" she asked with a groan.

"Maybe for the big one to come back," Jared replied.

Across the fire one of the goblins threw a wriggling black thing into the flames. "They never burn," the goblin said. "I wish they would burn."

"You still couldn't eat 'em," said another.

A soft voice from Jared's hood reminded him that Thimbletack was still with them. "Take a gander," whispered the brownie, "salamander."

Jared looked near his legs. One of the lizardlike things was next to his shoe. It was an opalescent black, with front legs and a long body that tapered to a tail. It was swallowing what appeared to be the tail of another.

"Jared," Mallory said. "Look in the fire. What are they?"

He leaned forward as far as his bonds would let him. There in the flames were all of the salamanders he'd seen the goblins toss. But instead of being scorched, they were sitting calmly as the blaze burned around them. As Jared stared, a few of the creatures moved slightly, one twisting its head and another scuttling deeper into the blaze. They really were immune to the fire.

He tried to think back to Arthur's Guide. He thought there was something on salamanders, but the images blurred in his mind. These little creatures looked like another illustration, but he couldn't quite put his finger on it. He was too nervous to concentrate — too full of thoughts of his mother and brother and of the goblins so close by.

A few moments later one of the goblins scurried over and poked Jared's stomach with a dirty claw. "They look so tasty. I could bite off one whole rosy cheek. I bet it would be sweet as candy." A long line of drool hit the dirt next to Jared.

Jared swallowed and looked over at Hogsqueal. The hobgoblin was using the dwarven sword to poke at the fire. He didn't look up, and that made Jared even more nervous.

Another goblin followed Jared's glance. "Wormrat will think he did it," the goblin said, pointing to Hogsqueal. "He was making a fuss before."

Hogsqueal stood up. "Of all the monkey-toasted, cracker-jack-headed . . ."

A third goblin approached, running its tongue over jagged teeth. "So much meat."

"Get away from him!" Mallory said. She pulled her hand out of Jared's. Only then did Jared realize he'd been clutching Mallory so tightly that his fingernails had dug into her skin.

"Would you rather we ate *you* instead?" asked the goblin sweetly. "Sugar and spice and everything nice. If that's what little girls are made of . . . sounds tasty to me!"

"Eat this!" Mallory said. She pulled her hands free and punched him in the face.

"The sword!" Jared yelled to Hogsqueal, trying to work his wrists out of the rope. The hobgoblin glanced at Jared once, then dropped the dwarven sword and ran from the clearing.

"Coward!" Jared yelled furiously. Free of his bindings, he ran toward the fire, but two goblins grabbed hold of his legs and toppled him into the dirt. Crawling forward until his hand could reach the blade, Jared swung the sword hilt-first to his sister. His hand stung, and he realized with dazed fascination that he had cut himself. More goblins jumped onto his back, pinning him in the dirt.

"Get away from him!" Mallory advanced, sword flashing as she swung it through the air. The goblins backed away from her. She whipped the blade at them. The goblins leaped off Jared and scrambled for their own weapons.

"Go! Run!" she yelled. A goblin jumped on her back, biting her shoulder.

Jared grabbed the goblin's arm and tugged it off his sister. Mallory kicked another that

"Get away from him!"

was approaching. One of the goblins picked up a dwarf-forged pike and swung it at Mallory. She parried it and then lunged, stabbing the goblin with her blade. As the creature howled, Mallory froze, realizing what she'd done. Blood stained the silver sword. The goblin fell, but others were rushing up fast and Mallory was still staring.

A screech above them broke her trance. Byron swooped toward the clearing and the goblins scattered, diving underneath trash for cover. The griffin's wings beat heavily, making the dirt dance.

"Come on," Jared said, grabbing at Mallory's arm. Together they leaped onto the rusted hood of a station wagon and then jumped down into a narrow path of corroded fencing. They ran past an overturned bathtub and a stack of tires. A series of doors were leaned up against a refrigerator, and as they passed them, Jared stopped abruptly. There, lying on a carpet of corrugated metal, was a cow.

It was a massive structure.

Chapter Five

IN WHICH They Find the Meaning of "Here There Be Dragons"

By reflex, Jared looked behind him, but the goblins were no longer there. The griffin landed with a clatter of claws on top of a car, denting it, and immediately began to groom himself like a cat. Simon grinned from Byron's back.

Jared turned to Mallory, but she was staring at the cow. It was chained to the ground, lowing softly, eyes wide enough to show the whites. Her udder was covered in what appeared to be writhing black snakes jostling for a position at her reddened teats. They blackened the metal sheeting on the ground beneath her like a squirming carpet. After a moment Jared realized the creatures were larger salamanders.

"What are those things doing?" Mallory asked. The bloodstained sword hung limply from her hand, and Jared was overwhelmed with the impulse to take it from her and clean it before she'd have a chance to notice.

He stepped closer to the cow instead. "Drinking the milk, I think."

"Ugh," Simon said, squinting down from Byron's back. "Weird."

Several more salamanders were lying in the dirt, their scales dull and their bodies wriggling. They were far larger than the tiny finger-length ones Jared and Mallory had seen in the fire.

"They're shedding their skin," Simon said. "What *are* they?"

Jared shook his head. "Fire-resistant salamanders. But they aren't supposed to get big like this. They look almost like . . ." But he wasn't quite sure what it was they reminded him of. Something nagged at the back of his mind.

At that moment Byron darted forward and seized one of the wriggling black creatures in his beak, tossed it into the air, and gulped it down. Then he seized another and another.

Greedily he went for an even larger one, as long as Jared's arm, curled up in the sun. It turned and hissed, and suddenly Jared knew what he was looking at.

"They're dragons," he said. "They're all dragons."

Out of the corner of his eye Jared saw something moving toward them, fast as a whip. He whirled, but the black thing hit him hard in the chest. Falling backward, he only had time to throw his hands up over his face before the thick body of a dragon as long as a couch scrabbled over him. Jared's head struck the ground, and for a moment everything went hazy.

"Jared!" Mallory howled. The dragon opened its mouth to show hundreds of teeth,

thin as needles. Jared froze. He was too terrified to move. His skin burned where the slick body had touched him.

Mallory chopped hard with her sword, catching the dragon's tail. Black blood spurted as the dragon turned toward her.

Jared got to his feet, dizzy and shivering. His skin was reddened, and the cut he'd gotten earlier throbbed angrily. "Watch out," he called. "It's poisonous!"

"Byron!" Simon yelled, pointing toward the black shape that was hurtling after Mallory. "Byron! Get it!"

The griffin swung up into the air with a screech. Jared looked after Byron and Simon desperately. How would Mallory escape the dragon now? She was cutting and thrusting as best as she could, but the dragon was too fast. Its body coiled and leaped like a snake, small forearms clutching and gripping, mouth so wide it seemed like it could swallow her whole. Mallory couldn't last. Jared had to do something.

Jared grabbed the nearest thing—a piece of metal—and hurled it at the dragon. The creature spun again and started toward him, lightning fast, jaws open. It hissed.

The griffin streaked down from the sky, talons reaching for the dragon, beak ripping at its back. The dragon coiled around Byron, wrapping its tail tight enough to choke. Simon hung on desperately as the griffin's wings

The dragon coiled around Byron.

THE DRAGON

pushed them back up into the air. The dragon twisted, teeth sinking into Byron's feathered and furred body. Then the griffin's wings missed a beat, and in the sudden drop, Simon slipped off.

Jared ran toward his twin as he plummeted toward the junkyard. Simon fell onto a pile of screen windows and his left arm twisted at an odd angle.

"Simon?" Jared knelt down beside him.

Simon moaned softly and used his other arm to push himself into a sitting position. His left cheek and neck were red from dragon poison, but the rest of his skin looked far too pale.

"Are you okay?" Jared whispered. Mallory touched Simon's arm gingerly.

Simon winced and stood up shakily. Above them the dragon and griffin were locked together, a writhing, looping knot of scales and skin. The dragon's teeth were embedded deep in Byron's neck, and the griffin was flying erratically.

"He's going to die." Simon limped toward the cow with her mass of dragon fingerlings.

"What are you doing?" Jared called after him.

When Simon turned back to them, tears were running down his face. As Jared watched him, Simon—who had never killed anything, who always carried spiders outside—stepped on the head of one of the baby dragons, crushing it into a smear under his shoe. It squealed. Dragon blood stained the ground and melted the edge of Simon's heel.

"Look!" he screamed. "Look what I'm doing to your babies!

The dragon turned in midair, and Byron seized the opportunity. Plunging his beak into

the creature's neck, he rent it wide. The dragon went limp in Byron's claws.

"Simon! You did it!" Mallory said.

Simon watched Byron land near them. His feathers were smeared with blood, and he shook himself. Then, dropping the body of the large dragon, Byron resumed eating the babies.

"This isn't going the way we planned," Simon said.

"But we're closer to the palace now," Jared said. "Mom has to be there."

"Do you think you can make it, Simon?" Mallory asked, although she didn't look very well herself, with her cheek cut and her jacket slashed at the shoulder.

Simon nodded, his face grim. "I can, but I don't know about Byron."

"We have to leave him here," Jared said. "I

think he'll be okay. The poison doesn't seem to affect him."

Byron gulped down another squirming black salamander and regarded the Grace kids with his strange golden eyes. Simon petted him carefully on the nose. "Yeah, he seems to like these dragons more than anything I used to feed him."

"Let me see if I can do something about your arm," Mallory said. "I think it's broken." She used her undershirt to tie Simon's arm neatly against his side.

"Are you sure you know what you're doing?" Simon asked, wincing.

"Sure I'm sure," Mallory said, tying the white fabric tight.

They marched in the direction of the palace. It was a massive structure made of what looked like cement or stucco, mixed with gravel, glass, and aluminum cans. It looked less molded than poured and in some places resembled dried lava. The windows were strangely shaped, as though the creator had fitted the house around whatever refuse he had found. Lights flickered inside. Several spires came to delicate points off the main roof, which was black with tar and covered in overlapping layers of glass and tin that looked like fish scales. As Jared got closer, he noticed that the main gate was made of old brass headboards. Beyond the gate was a deep trench dug in the earth, studded with jagged, rusty metal and chunks of broken glass. The drawbridge was down.

"Shouldn't there be goblins guarding it or something?" Mallory asked.

The drawbridge was down.

Jared looked around. In the distance he could see tendrils of smoke coming from what he guessed were goblin camps.

"It's going to be dark soon," Simon said.

"It just seems too easy," Jared said. "Like a trap."

"Trap or not, we're going to have to keep going," Mallory said.

Simon nodded. Jared still thought that Simon looked a little too pale and wondered how much pain he was in. At least the red skin had faded somewhat.

Stepping onto the drawbridge cautiously, Jared braced himself for something to happen. He kept glancing at the jagged glass jutting up out of the moat. Then he raced across. Mallory and Simon paused a moment, then ran after him.

As they entered the palace, they found

themselves in a large hall constructed from salvaged materials and what seemed to be cement. The archways were trimmed with bent chrome fenders. Hubcaps hung from the ceiling on rusted chains, flickering with the uncertain light of dozens of yellowed candles and dripping with wax. Set inside one wall was a fireplace large enough to roast Jared in.

It was eerily quiet. Their footsteps echoed in the dim rooms, and their shadows loomed along the walls.

They walked farther, passing musty-smelling couches covered in threadbare throws.

"Do we have anything even remotely resembling a plan?" Mallory asked.

"Nope," Jared said.

"No," Simon echoed.

"Hush," said Thimbletack. "Have a care. I hear something over there."

They paused a moment, listening. There was a faint noise that sounded almost like music.

"I think it's coming from here," Jared said, pushing open a door that had been decorated with more than a dozen knobs. Inside the room was a tall, long table made from a plank of wood on top of three sawhorses. Thick candles that smelled of burning hair covered most of the table. Rivulets of melted wax ran down the sides. Also set on the table were platters of food—long, greasy trays of roasted frogs, half-eaten apples, the tail and

bones of a large fish. Flies buzzed greedily around the remains. From somewhere in the room came a series of high-pitched notes.

"What is that?" Simon asked, squeezing past a single large chair. Then he stopped, looking at something Jared and Mallory couldn't see. They scrambled over to him.

A large urn sat on the floor underneath an open window. There, in the wavering light, Jared could see sprites trapped in honey, sinking as though it were quicksand. The sprites' tiny cries were the sound he had heard before.

Simon reached in to pull the sprites free, but the honey was heavy and clung to their thin wings, tearing them. The sprites squealed as he set each one down on the table in a sticky, sodden heap. One was completely still and lay there limply, like a doll. Jared looked away, staring out the window.

"Do you think there are more in there?" Mallory whispered.

"I think so," Simon said. "At the bottom."

"We have to keep going." Jared moved toward another doorway. The thought of the tiny drowned faeries made him feel queasy.

"The palace is just too quiet," said Mallory as she followed him.

"Mulgarath can't be here all the time," Jared said. "Maybe we got lucky. Maybe we can just find Mom and get out."

Mallory nodded, but she didn't look convinced.

They passed by a map hung on a wall. It looked much like Arthur's old map, but the places had been renamed. Jared noticed that over the junkyard had been written MULGARATH'S PALACE and that lettered across the entire top of the paper was MULGARATH'S DOMAIN.

"Look!" Simon said. Ahead of them was a large room with a throne at its center. Surrounding the throne were overlapping carpets in different patterns, all of them moth-eaten and worn. The throne was made of metal, welded together and jagged in places.

At one end of the room was a spiral staircase, each step a plank suspended on two long metal chains. The whole thing looked like a web, wobbling slightly with each breeze. In the dim light the stairs looked impossible to climb.

Mallory pulled herself onto the first rung. It swung alarmingly. She tried to step onto the next one, but her legs were too short.

"These steps are too far apart!" she exclaimed.

"Perfect for an ogre," Simon pointed out.

She finally managed to catch the second step, flop onto it chest-first, and pull herself up that way.

The stairs looked impossible to climb.

"Simon's not going to be able to climb this," she said.

"I can . . . I'll be okay," Simon insisted, lifting himself awkwardly onto the first step.

Mallory shook her head. "You're going to fall."

"Hold on tight," Thimbletack called from Jared's hood. "You'll be all right." Then Jared watched in amazement as each step swung closer and held steady for his siblings to climb onto it. With one working arm and Mallory's help, Simon climbed up the stairs.

"It would behoove you to move," said Thimbletack.

"Oh, right." Jared worked his way up the steps. Even with the brownie's help, his heart thundered as he went higher and higher. The cut on his hand burned where he gripped the chains. Glancing down into the darkness below made Jared momentarily dizzy.

At the top they found themselves in a hall-way with three doors, all mismatched.

"Let's try the middle one," Simon said.

"We made so much noise just now," said Mallory. "Where is everyone? It's eerie."

"We have to keep going," Jared said, repeating his words from earlier.

Mallory sighed and opened the door. It opened onto a large room with a balcony made of mismatched stones and chains. Giant cathedral windows, filled with translucent mosaics made of glass shards, covered the other wall. Their mother was in one corner, bound, gagged, and unconscious. In the other corner, hanging from ropes and a pulley, was their dad.

"What are you doing here?"

Chapter Six

IN WHICH All Hell Breaks Loose

What are you doing here?" Jared asked. Behind him he heard Simon and Mallory exclaim "Dad!" together. Their father's black hair looked slightly mussed and his shirt was untucked on one side, but it was definitely him.

Their father's eyes went wide. "Jared! Simon! Mallory! Thank goodness you're okay."

Jared furrowed his brow. Something about this didn't feel right. He looked around the room again. Out beyond the balcony he saw goblins milling in the gloom, holding torches. What was going on?

"Quick," Mallory said. "We have to move. Jared, untie Mom. I'll work on Dad."

Jared leaned down and touched his mother's pale cheek. It felt cold and clammy. Her glasses were gone. "Mom's unconscious," he said.

"Is she breathing?" Mallory asked, halting.

Jared put his hand against his mother's lips and felt the ghost of her breath. "She's okay. She's alive."

"Did you see Mulgarath?" Simon asked his father. "The ogre?"

"There was some commotion outside," Mr. Grace said. "I didn't see anything after that."

Mallory fumbled with the pulley and managed to lower her dad's hands. "How did they get you all the way from California?"

Their dad shook his head wearily. "Your mother called to say how worried she was—all three of you acting strange and then going missing. I came as soon as I could, but the monsters were already at the house. It was terrible. At first I couldn't believe what was happening. And they kept talking about a book. What is this book?"

"Our uncle Arthur—" Jared began.

"More like Mom's great-uncle, our great-great-uncle," Mallory said as she picked at the knots.

"Right. Well, he was interested in faeries." Jared untied his mother as he talked, but even free from her bonds, she didn't move. Jared smoothed back her hair, wishing she would open her eyes.

"His brother got eaten by a troll," Simon put in.

RICHARD GRACE

Jared nodded, looking nervously around. How long before they were discovered? Did they really have time for this? Now that they had found their mother, they had to get out as quickly as possible. "And so he made this book that was all about faeries. It had stuff in it that even some of the faeries themselves didn't know."

"Because they mostly don't bother with one another, it seems," Mallory said.

How were they going to get their mother down the stairs? Could their dad carry her? Jared tried to concentrate on explaining. They had to make sure their dad would understand. "But the faeries didn't want one guy to have that much power over them, so they tried to get the book back. When he wouldn't give it to them, they took him instead."

"The elves did," Simon said.

"Really?" said their father with a strange gleam in his eye.

Jared sighed. "Look, I know it sounds unbelievable, Dad, but look around. Does this look like the set of one of your movies?"

"I believe you," their father said softly.

"To make a very long story short," Mallory said, "we found the book."

"Except we lost the book again," said Simon. "The ogre has it."

"And he's got a really idiotic plan to take over the world," Mallory put in.

Their father's eyebrows rose, but he only

said, "So, now that the book is gone, all of the knowledge is gone with it. There's no other copy? That seems like a shame."

"Jared remembers a lot," Simon said. "I bet he could make a book of his own."

Mallory nodded. "And we learned some stuff along the way—right, Jared?"

Jared smiled, looking down. "I guess so," he said finally. "But I wish I remembered more."

Their father flexed his newly freed wrists and stretched his legs. "I'm sorry that I wasn't here sooner. I shouldn't have left you kids and your mom alone. And I want to make it up to you. I want to stay."

"We missed you too, Dad," Simon said.

Mallory looked down at her boots. "Yeah."

Jared said nothing. Something about this was too easy. It just felt wrong. "Mom?" he said softly, and shook her.

Dad spread his arms wide. "Come and give your father a hug."

Simon and Mallory embraced him. Jared looked down at his mother and reluctantly started to cross the room, when his dad said, "I want us all to be together from now on."

Jared froze. He wanted it so much to be true, but it didn't feel true. "Dad would never say that," he said.

His father grabbed hold of his arm. "Don't you *want* us to be a family again?"

"Of course I do!" Jared yelled, jerking his arm free and stepping back. "I want Dad to be less of a jerk, and for Mom to not be sad. I want my dad to stop talking about himself and his movies and his life all the time and remember that I'm the loser who almost got kicked out of school and Simon is the one who likes animals and Mallory is the fencer. But that's not going to happen and *you're not him.*"

As Jared looked up into the familiar hazel eyes of his father, they started to turn pale yellow. His father's body elongated, filling out, becoming a mammoth shape clad in the tattered remains of ancient finery. His hands became claws, and his dark hair twined together into branches. "Mulgarath," Jared said.

The ogre wrapped one arm around Mallory's neck and with the other arm grabbed Simon.

"Come here, Jared Grace!" Mulgarath's voice boomed, far deeper than their father's. He strode toward the balcony, still holding Simon and Mallory. "Give yourself up. Otherwise, I will heave your brother and sister into my moat of glass and iron."

"Leave them alone," Jared said shakily. "You have the book."

"You're not him".

"I can't do that," Mulgarath said. "You know the secret that speeds the growth of dragons and how to kill them. You know the weaknesses of my goblins. I cannot allow you to make another Guide."

"Run!" Mallory yelled. "Get Mom and run!" She bit the ogre.

He laughed and pressed his arm tighter against her, heaving her up into the air. "Do you think your feeble strength is enough to match mine, human girl?"

Simon kicked, but the hulking monster didn't seem to notice.

A groan came from the other end of the room, and Jared half turned. His mother stirred and opened her eyes. They went wide. "Richard? I thought I heard . . . oh my God!"

"Everything's going to be okay, Mom," Jared said, wishing for his voice to stay even. Somehow her seeing all of this made it more horrible.

"Mom, tell him to run!" Mallory shouted. "Both of you! Go!"

"Quiet, girl, or I'll break your neck." The ogre growled, but when he addressed Jared, his voice became soothing. "It's a fair trade, isn't it? Your life for the lives of your brother and sister and mother?"

"Jared, what's happening?" their mother called.

Jared tried to stay calm. He was afraid to die, but it would be so much worse to watch his brother, sister, and mother get hurt. Already the ogre's fingers seemed to be loosening, ready to drop Simon and Mallory at any moment. "You won't free us — even if I promise not to make another Guide!"

Mulgarath shook his head slowly, eyes full of dark satisfaction.

"Put them down!" Their mother's voice was panicked. "Put my children down! Jared, what are you doing?"

It was then that Jared noticed Mallory's sword lying on the floor.

Seeing the sword made Jared focus. He had to concentrate—to come up with a plan. Jared remembered what Arthur had said about ogres—they liked to brag. He only hoped that this one would. "I'll give up and come over there."

"No, you idiot!" Mallory shouted.

"Jared, don't!" Simon yelled.

"But before I do . . ." Jared swallowed hard and hoped that the ogre would take the bait. "There's something I want to know. Why are you doing all of this? Why now?"

Mulgarath smiled toothily. "You humans take everything and keep the best part for

"Why are you doing all of this?"

yourselves. You live in palaces, dine on banquets, and clothe yourselves in fine silks and velvets like royalty. We, who live forever, who have magic, who have *power,* are supposed to lie down and let your kind trample us into the ground. No more.

"I have been planning this for a long time. First I thought I would have to wait for my dragons to mature. I have time on my side. But with the Guide I was able to step up my plans. As long as they have enough milk, the dragons are quite docile, you know. And I am sure by now you've realized how fast the milk makes them grow and how powerful they become.

"The elves are too feeble to stop me, and the humans will never see it coming. It is my time—the time of Mulgarath! The time of goblins! The land will have a new master!"

Jared tipped his head to the side, hoping Mulgarath was too busy talking to notice, and whispered into his hood. "Thimbletack, can you make the chains on the railing attach to Mallory's and Simon's legs?"

Thimbletack wriggled and whispered back. "I'd have to get to the ground without making a sound."

"I'll keep him talking," Jared whispered, then raised his voice, addressing the ogre. "So why did you have to kill the dwarves? I don't understand. They wanted to help you."

"They had their own little dream of a world built of iron and gold. But what fun would it be to rule a world like that? No, I want a world of flesh and blood and bone." The ogre smiled again, as though pleased with the way that had sounded, then looked down at Jared. "Enough talk. Come here."

"What about the Guide?" Jared asked. "At least tell me where that is."

"I think not," Mulgarath said. "It is beyond you now."

"I just want to know if I could have found it," Jared said.

A cruel smile twisted the ogre's features. "Indeed, had you been more clever, you could have found it. A pity that you are a mere human child, no match for me at all. The book was beneath my throne this whole time."

"You know," Jared said, "we killed your dragons. I hope that doesn't put too much of a dent in your clever plan."

Mulgarath looked genuinely surprised. Then his brow knotted with anger.

Out of the corner of his eye Jared could see the chains unlinking and snaking across the floor like vipers. One wrapped around

Mallory's leg, and the other circled Simon's waist. When the metal touched her skin, Mallory flinched. A third chain crept toward Mulgarath's ankle, and Jared hoped that the ogre would not notice.

But Jared's pause was enough to catch Mulgarath's attention. He looked down and spotted Thimbletack skittering along the floor. The ogre kicked the brownie, his giant foot tossing Thimbletack across the room, where Thimbletack landed like a crumpled glove beside Mrs. Grace. The chains stopped moving. "What is this?" Mulgarath bellowed, stamping down on the links near his foot. "You sought to trick me?"

Jared ran forward and grabbed Mallory's silver sword.

Mulgarath laughed and dropped Simon and
Mallory off the side of the balcony. They both
screamed and then were silent, while their
mother's scream went on and on. Jared didn't
know if the chains had held. He didn't know
anything.

Jared thought he might be sick. Rage filled
him. Everything looked small and far away. He
felt the weight of the sword in his hand as though
it were the only real thing in the world. He raised
it high. Someone far away was calling his name,
but he didn't care. Nothing mattered anymore.

Then just as he was about to swing, he saw
the look of satisfaction on the ogre's face — as if
Jared were doing just what Mulgarath had
expected . . . as if Jared were playing right into
his hands. If he swung the sword, he would be
matching his strength against the ogre's, and
the ogre would win.

Abruptly Jared changed the direction of his blow and brought the point of the sword down hard, stabbing Mulgarath in the foot.

The ogre howled with surprise and pain, lifting his wounded foot. Jared dropped the sword and grabbed the chain that ran beneath the ogre's other foot, pulling with his full weight. Mulgarath stumbled backward, trying to regain his balance. But just as his calves hit the chain fence, Jared slammed into him again. The ogre's weight pulled the chains loose from the wall, and he went hurtling over the side.

Jared rushed to the edge of the balcony. To his immense relief, Simon and Mallory were dangling over the pit, chains wrapped around Simon's waist and Mallory's leg. They called up to him weakly.

Jared started to smile, but as he did, he saw Mulgarath, his fist clutching another chain, his body shifting into the shape of a squirming dragon. He began to writhe his way back up to them.

"Watch out!" Jared shouted.

Simon, hanging closer to the monster, tried to kick at it. He only made the chains swing dangerously.

Mallory and Simon screamed as Jared leaned out as far as he could and swung the sword again. This time it hit the ogre's chain, cutting through it and biting into the wall of the palace. Mulgarath started to transform once more. As the ogre fell toward the pit of jagged glass, his body became smaller and smaller until he finally became a swallow. The bird veered out of the pit, heading toward the assembled throng of goblins. In mere moments Mulgarath would lead that army into the palace. There would be no escape for the Grace family.

But then, as the bird turned, angling to fly back toward where the children stood, a hobgoblin's hand suddenly shot out and grabbed the bird out of the air. It happened so fast that Jared didn't have time to be surprised and the ogre didn't have time to shift again.

Hogsqueal bit off the bird's head and chewed twice with apparent enjoyment. "Cruddy mouth-breather," he said as he gulped it down.

Jared couldn't help it. He started to laugh.

"All this time and I never knew."

Epilogue

IN WHICH the Story of the Grace Children Comes to Its Conclusion

Jared sat down on the gleaming floor of Arthur's newly cleaned library and leaned against Aunt Lucinda's leg. Mallory knelt next to him, making stacks of old letters written in languages that none of them spoke. Simon flipped through an old book of sepia photographs while their mother poured hot tea into mugs.

All of that might have seemed normal if Hogsqueal wasn't seated on a nearby footstool, playing checkers with a bandaged and annoyed-looking Thimbletack.

Lucinda held up one of the paintings of the little girl from Arthur's desk. "I can't believe it. All this time and I never knew."

It had been three weeks since they had defeated Mulgarath, and Jared was finally starting to think things were going to *stay* okay. The goblins had dispersed into bickering groups. Byron was gone by the time they had left the palace, and he appeared to have eaten every last dragonet. Jared, Simon, Mallory, and their mother had all walked home from the dump. It had been a long walk, and they had been so tired that once they'd arrived home, they had collapsed into the piles of feathers and cloth that had been their beds without complaint or comment. It was dark when Jared had finally woken and noticed Thimbletack curled up on a pillow beside him, with Simon's tiny, marmalade cat nestled against the little brownie. Jared had smiled, taken a deep breath, and choked on the feathers.

Downstairs he'd found his mother cleaning up the kitchen. When Jared had walked into the room, she had hugged him tightly.

"I'm so sorry," she'd said.

Even though it had kind of made him feel like a baby, he'd hugged her back for a long time.

Later that week their mother had arranged for Lucinda to leave the asylum and come stay with them. Jared had been amazed to find his great-aunt, with a haircut and a new suit, sitting in the parlor one day after school. When Mulgarath died, his magic must have died with him, and although Lucinda often walked with a cane now, her back was as straight as it had ever been.

Mrs. Grace had been less miraculous in curing Jared's school troubles; he had been expelled. His mother had enrolled him and Simon in a private school nearby. She claimed the school had excellent art and science programs. Mallory decided to stay at the old school. She only had one year till she was in high school anyway and plenty still to prove to the J. Waterhouse fencing team.

For his part, Jared had locked Arthur's field guide in its metal trunk again. But after all that he still didn't know what to think. Were there creatures still after them? Had the ogre been the worst—or just the worst yet?

A breeze blew through the office, scattering papers and snapping Jared out of his thoughts. Simon jumped up, trying to catch hold of the letters.

"Did you leave a window open?" their mother asked Aunt Lucinda.

"I don't recall doing so," their great-aunt replied.

"I'll get it," Mallory said, and started toward the window.

Then a single leaf blew inside. It danced in the air, swooping and swirling, until it fell directly in front of Jared. The leaf was greenish brown, and Jared thought it might be from a maple tree. Written on the leaf in a delicate hand was Jared's name. He turned it over and read:

The time has come
Meet us tonight
under the full moon
Bring the book

"It doesn't say where," Mallory said, reading over his shoulder.

"The grove, I guess," Jared said.

"You're not going to go, are you?" Simon asked.

"I'm going," said Jared. "I promised. I need to give them Arthur's field guide. I don't want anything like this to happen again."

"Then we're going with you," said Simon.

"I'm coming too," their mother said.

The three children looked at her with surprise, then glanced at each other.

"Don't forget me, dizzinits," Hogsqueal said.

"Don't forget *us*," Thimbletack corrected.

Aunt Lucy reached for her cane. "I hope it isn't much of a walk?"

That night they left the house carrying lanterns, flashlights, and the field guide. It was weird to go looking for faeries with their mother in tow and Simon helping Aunt Lucy along. Up the hill they went, and then they carefully made their way down the other side.

Jared thought he heard a whisper of "Clever is as clever does," but it might have been only his memory or the wind.

The grove was lit with dozens upon dozens of sprites, whirring through the air, twinkling like giant fireflies, alighting on tree branches and settling in the grass. Elves sat on the ground—many more than the three the children had seen on their first visit—all clad in the deep colors of autumn as though to camouflage themselves with the forest.

The elves went quiet as the small group of humans made their way to the center of the clearing. There, standing among all of those seated, was the green-eyed elf, her expression unreadable. Beside her stood the leaf-horned elf, looking stern, and red-haired Lorengorm, who was smiling.

Thinking of Thimbletack, Jared made an awkward bow. The others followed his example.

"We brought the book," Jared said, and held it out to the green-eyed elf.

She smiled. "That is well. We must abide by our promises, and had you not, Simon would have had to stay with us for a very long time."

Simon shivered and stepped closer to Mallory. Jared scowled.

"But since you have done so," she continued, "we wish to return it to you for safekeeping."

"What?" Mallory said. Jared was astonished.

"You have proven that humans may use the

knowledge it contains for good. Therefore we return the Guide to you."

Lorengorm stepped forward. "We also wish to give you some measure of our gratitude for restoring peace to these lands. To that end we offer you a boon."

"A boon?" Hogsqueal puffed out his chest. "What do I get? How come these ninnyhammers get a reward when I'm the one that defeated Mulgarath?"

Several of the elves began to laugh, and Thimbletack gave Hogsqueal a stern look.

"Figures he wasn't coming along to be supportive," Mallory said.

"So what would you like, little hobgoblin?" asked the green-eyed elf.

"Well," Hogsqueal said, putting a finger to his mouth as if considering. "I'd like some kind of medal, definitely. Gold, with 'fearsome killer of ogres' on it. No, wait, how about 'supreme slayer of monsters'? Or—"

"Is that all?" asked Lorengorm.

"It should say 'supreme beetlehead,'" Simon whispered to Jared.

"I don't think so," said the hobgoblin. "I want a victory feast in my honor. And it should have quail's eggs — I love those — and pigeon baked in a pie shell and barbequed ca — "

"We'll consider your requests," the green-eyed elf said, barely hiding a smile behind her delicate hand. "But now I must ask the children to name the desire of their heart."

Jared looked at his brother and sister. At first they seemed thoughtful, and then smiles started to grow on their faces. Jared glanced back at his mother, who still seemed a bit confused, and his great-aunt, her face full of hope.

"We would like our great-great-uncle, Arthur Spiderwick, to have a choice whether to stay in Faerie or not."

"You understand," Lorengorm said, "that if he chooses to return to the mortal world, the

For my darling Lucy
- love Papa

Watercolor study of Arthur and Lucinda Spiderwick, found in Arthur's study.

first time his foot touches the earth, he will become dust and ash."

Jared nodded. "I understand."

"We have anticipated your request," said the green-eyed elf. With a wave of her hand the trees parted, and Byron stepped through. On his back was Arthur Spiderwick.

Jared heard the others gasp behind him. Arthur smiled at Jared briefly, and this time Jared noticed that his eyes were like Lucinda's, both sharp and kind. Arthur sat on the griffin awkwardly and petted him with a kind of awe. Then he looked over at Mallory and Simon. He adjusted his glasses.

"You are my great-great-niece and nephew, aren't you?" he said softly. "Jared didn't mention that he had a brother and a sister."

Jared nodded. He wondered if there was any way he could apologize for the things he

"This is fine work."

had said earlier. He wondered what Arthur thought of him.

"I'm Simon," said Simon. "This is Mallory, and this is our mom." Simon looked at Lucinda and hesitated.

"I'm glad to meet you," said Arthur. "You three children clearly have my inquisitive blood running through your veins. You might have had cause to regret it." He shook his head wryly. "It seems to have gotten you into a lot of scrapes. Luckily you three seem far more adept at getting yourselves out of trouble than I ever was." He smiled again, and this time his smile wasn't the least bit tentative. It was a wide grin that made him look very unlike the man in the painting.

"We're glad to see you too," Jared said. "We want to give your book back to you."

"My field guide!" Arthur said. He took it from Jared's hands and started flipping through it. "Look at this—who did these sketches?"

"I did," Jared said, his voice as soft as a whisper. "I know they aren't very good."

"Nonsense!" Arthur said. "This is fine work. I predict that you are going to be a great artist someday."

"Really?" Jared said.

Arthur nodded. "Really."

Thimbletack walked up to Arthur's shoes. "Good to see you, my old friend, but there are some things to mend. Here is Lucinda, who you know. She is not as she was long ago."

Arthur's breath caught as he finally recognized her. *She must look so old to him,* Jared thought. He tried to picture his mother as a young woman, looking at an elderly version of him, but it was too hard, too sad.

Lucinda smiled, and tears ran down her

cheeks. "Daddy!" she said. "You look just the way you did the day you left."

Arthur made a move to dismount.

"No!" Lucinda said. "You'll turn to dust." Leaning on her cane, she walked closer to where he stood.

"I'm sorry for all of the sadness I caused you and your mother," he said. "I'm sorry I tried to trick the elves. I should have never taken the risk. I've always loved you, Lucy. I always wanted to come home."

"You are home now," said Lucinda.

Arthur shook his head. "Elven magic has kept me alive too long. I have lived past the span of my years. It is my time to go, but seeing you, Lucy—I can go without sorrow."

"I just got you back," she said. "You can't die now."

Arthur bent down and spoke to her—soft

words that Jared could not hear—before he stepped off the griffin and into her embrace. As Arthur's foot touched the ground, his body turned to dust and then smoke. It swirled around Jared's great-aunt and then whirled up into the night sky and was gone.

Jared turned to Lucinda, expecting to see her crying, but her eyes were dry. She stared up at the stars and smiled. Jared slid his hand into hers.

"It's time for us to go home," Aunt Lucinda said. Jared nodded. He thought about everything that had happened, all of the things that he had seen, and suddenly realized how much he still had to sketch. After all, he was only at the beginning.

Here ends the tale of

THE GRACE
CHILDREN

About TONY DiTERLIZZI . . .

A *New York Times* best-selling author, Tony DiTerlizzi created the Zena Sutherland Award–winning *Ted, Jimmy Zangwow's Out-of-This-World Moon Pie Adventure,* as well as illustrations in Tony Johnston's Alien and Possum beginning-reader series. Most recently, his brilliantly cinematic version of Mary Howitt's classic *The Spider and the Fly* was awarded a Caldecott Honor. In addition, Tony's art has graced the work of such well-known fantasy names as J.R.R. Tolkien, Anne McCaffrey, Peter S. Beagle, and Greg Bear as well as Wizards of the Coast's *Magic The Gathering*. He and his wife, Angela, reside with their pug, Goblin, in Amherst, Massachusetts. Visit Tony on the World Wide Web at www.diterlizzi.com.

and HOLLY BLACK

An avid collector of rare folklore volumes, Holly Black spent her early years in a decaying Victorian mansion where her mother fed her a steady diet of ghost stories and books about faeries. Accordingly, her first novel, *Tithe: A Modern Faerie Tale*, is a gothic and artful glimpse at the world of Faerie. Published in the fall of 2002, it received two starred reviews and a Best Book for Young Adults citation from the American Library Association. She lives in West Long Branch, New Jersey, with her husband, Theo, and a remarkable menagerie. Visit Holly on the World Wide Web at www.blackholly.com.

Tony and Holly continue to work day and night fending off angry faeries and goblins in order to bring the Grace children's story to you.

Through field, cave, and forest
this yarn has unspun
with our heroes victorious
and evil undone!

Yet all is not merry
as we reach this end
and must bid farewell
to a father, guide, . . . friend.

Though Arthur is taken,
what's given is vast!
His beloved Lucinda
is safe home at last.

JARED GRACE

SIMON GRACE

Hogsqueal has eaten.
The Graces can rest.
And Thimbletack's back to
what brownies do best.

With everyone happy
and no longer vexed,
one question needs answering. . . .
What happens next?

MALLORY GRACE

THIMBLETACK

Are there more ogres
and dragons to slay?
Is there more mayhem,
perhaps, on the way?

TONY DITERLIZZI

Ask Tony and Holly.
They'll swear that it's true.
But you still won't believe
what's coming for you!

For the time is upon us.
The Guide is at hand.
Soon Spiderwick's opus
will be read through the land.

HOLLY BLACK

So keep your eyes open.
And when you see it, do choose it!
Because knowledge is good. . . .
Just beware how you use it.

ACKNOWLEDGMENTS

Tony and Holly would like to thank
Steve and Dianna for their insight,
Starr for her honesty,
Myles and Liza for sharing the journey,
Ellen and Julie for helping make this our reality,
Kevin for his tireless enthusiasm and faith in us,
and especially Angela and Theo—
there are not enough superlatives
to describe your patience
in enduring endless nights
of Spiderwick discussion.

The text type for this book is set in Cochin.
The display types are set in Nevins Hand and Rackham.
The illustrations are rendered in pen and ink.
Production editor: Dorothy Gribbin
Art director: Dan Potash
Production manager: Chava Wolin